W9-CDG-976

DEAR TITIEZ,

CAN YOU BELIEVE IT?? I MET ANTHONY BROWNE IN PERSON!! THIS IS HIS LATEST PICTURE BOOK & IT'S JUST SO AMAZING! I CAN GUARANTEE THAT EVERY TIME YOU READ THIS, YOU WILL NOTICE SOMETHING NEW! HE IS JUST BRILLIANT! ANYWAYS, YOU WERE THE FIRST PERSON I THOUGHT OF! YOU ARE WRITTEN ALL OVER IT! I HOPE YOU ENJOY IT AS MUCH AS I DO.

♡ STEPH

P.S. WE ARE 'THE TWO FRIDAS' xxxx

15th MAY 2019
LONDON

To all the little Fridas in the world

First published 2019 by Walker Books Ltd, 87 Vauxhall Walk, London SE11 5HJ

2 4 6 8 10 9 7 5 3 1

© 2019 Anthony Browne

The right of Anthony Browne to be identified as author/illustrator of this work has been
asserted by him in accordance with the Copyright, Designs and Patents Act 1988

This book has been typeset in Plantin
Printed in China

All rights reserved. No part of this book may be reproduced, transmitted or stored in an information
retrieval system in any form or by any means, graphic, electronic or mechanical, including
photocopying, taping and recording, without prior written permission from the publisher.

British Library Cataloguing in Publication Data: a catalogue record for
this book is available from the British Library

ISBN 978-1-4063-8122-1

www.walker.co.uk

For Tiffany

Anthony Browne.

Little Frida

ANTHONY BROWNE

WALKER BOOKS
AND SUBSIDIARIES
LONDON · BOSTON · SYDNEY · AUCKLAND

When I was six I fell ill with polio and had to stay in bed for nine months. It was extremely painful and when I eventually got better I could only walk slowly, with a limp. Other children laughed and made fun of me, calling me "Peg-Leg!" whenever I walked past.

I tried to hide my thin right leg with three layers of socks, but it didn't fool anybody.

I was different and being different made me an outsider.

My father was a photographer and
sometimes he let me help him in his studio.
I coloured up many of his black-and-white
photographs. Although it was boring work
I loved being together with him.

Most days though, in spite of having
three sisters, I played on my own. I was
lonely, but I quite liked being separate.

When I slept I dreamed of flying. I longed to really fly.

I thought about it all the time and for my seventh birthday

I asked my parents for a toy plane. For days I could think

of nothing else but flying right around the world…

But when the day finally came, these wings were all I got…

I didn't want to show my disappointment so I kept

the stupid wings on and ran to my room.

As I breathed on the window it slowly became

misty with condensation. I idly drew a shape on the

glass with my finger. Then I added a handle,

and suddenly it was a door!

I opened the door, and stepped through it. I was FREE.

I could run!

I ran and ran and ran until I was completely exhausted.

I was hot and very thirsty and there in

front of me was a dairy. I walked all round

the building looking for a way in but

I couldn't see one.

Just when I was about to give up and go home

I noticed a little door. I crawled inside.

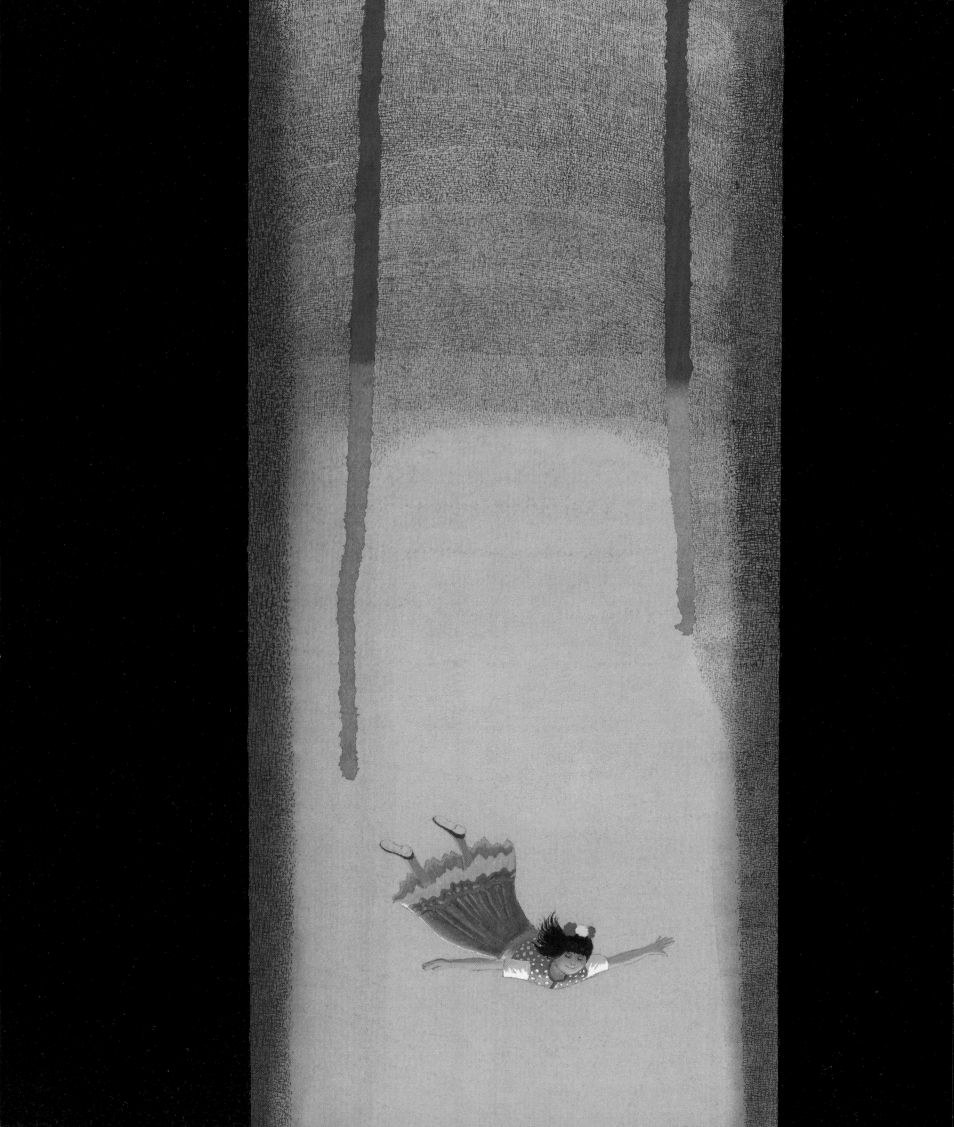

And then

I seemed

to be falling

slowly

down into

the depths

of the earth.

At the bottom a girl was waiting for me. She didn't say anything, not even "Hello", but in a strange way I felt as if I'd known her all my life.

I smiled at her and she smiled too.

The girl silently started to dance. She was a beautiful dancer and while she gracefully danced around the room I talked to her. I told her all the secret things I worried about (there were many), and she listened to every word I said.

The girl was a stranger, but she felt so familiar. We sat and laughed together. I laughed very loudly and she laughed without making a sound. We quickly became the closest friends.

I'd never had a friend before.
It was a wonderful feeling.

After a while I knew I had to go. We waved goodbye

and I flew back home, away from the dairy …

across the plains, and through the door drawn on

the window. I rubbed out the door and ran to the

furthest corner of the garden.

I sat there and thought about my
journey and my new friend.
I was alone again, but now I was
very happy. I knew that I could
go back and see her whenever
I wanted. She would be there
waiting for me.

From that day I began to paint
the girl, over and over again.
I've visited her many times since
that day, and in a way, I've been
painting her ever since…